NICKI WEISS

DOG·BOY·CAP·SKATE

GREENWILLOW BOOKS NEW YORK

GOUACHE PAINTS WERE USED FOR THE FULL-COLOR ART.
THE TEXT TYPE IS ITC USHERWOOD.

PRINTED IN SINGAPORE BY TIEN WAH PRESS
FIRST EDITION   10 9 8 7 6 5 4 3 2 1

LIBRARY OF CONGRESS CATALOGING-IN-PUBLICATION DATA

WEISS, NICKI.
DOG BOY CAP SKATE / BY NICKI WEISS.
P.   CM.
SUMMARY: A BOY ICE SKATES WHILE HIS DOG WATCHES.
ISBN 0-688-08275-0.
ISBN 0-688-08276-9 (LIB. BDG.)
[1. ICE SKATING—FICTION.   2. DOGS—FICTION.
3. STORIES IN RHYME.]   I. TITLE.
PZ8.3.W425DO   1989
[E]—DC19   88-16390   CIP   AC

FOR
PEGGY
MICHAEL
JESSICA
AND ZOE

Dog   Boy

Cap   Skate

Snow   Scarf

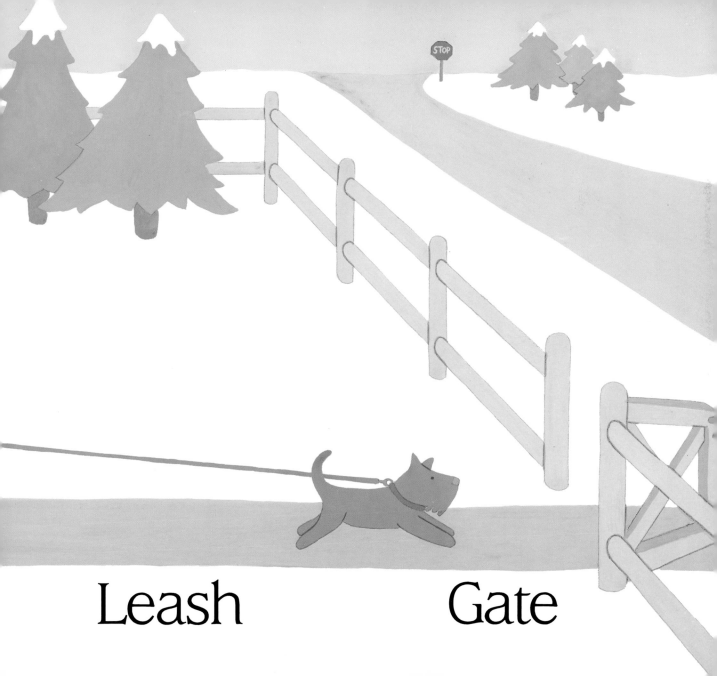

Leash   Gate

Hill   Sled

Pond   Park

Friend   Smile

Friend   Bark

Bench   Boot

Knot   Lace

Spin   Jump

Circle   Race

Step

Step

Slip   Slide

Fall

Kneel

Wobble Glide

North   South

East   West

Spin

Jump

Circle

Rest

Sit   Slump

Sigh   Sag

Hand   Help

Hold   Wag

Pull   Scrape

Push   Slow

Slide Glide

Together...

Go!